FROM OUR OWN FIRE

William Letford published his first collection of poetry while working as a roofer. Since then, his work has been adapted into film, projected onto buildings, carved into monuments, adapted for the stage, written onto skin, cast out over the radio, and performed by orchestras. He has helped restore a medieval village in the mountains of northern Italy, taught English in Japan, fished with his barehands in Indonesia, and been invited to perform in Iraq, South Korea, Lebanon, Australia, Germany, India, Poland, and many more countries.

From Our Own Fire

WILLIAM LETFORD

CARCANET POETRY

First published in Great Britain in 2023 by
Carcanet
Alliance House, 30 Cross Street
Manchester, M2 7AQ
www.carcanet.co.uk

A CIP catalogue record for this book is
available from the British Library.

ISBN 978 1 80017 343 9

Book design by Andrew Latimer, Carcanet
Typesetting by LiteBook Prepress Services
Printed in Great Britain by SRP Ltd, Exeter, Devon

The publisher acknowledges financial
assistance from Arts Council England.

for Layton, River, Eban, and Willow

The primitive forms of artificial intelligence we already have, have proved very useful. But I think the development of full artificial intelligence could spell the end of the human race. Once humans develop artificial intelligence, it would take off on its own and redesign itself at an ever-increasing rate. Humans who are limited by slow biological evolution couldn't compete and would be superseded.

STEPHEN HAWKING

CONTENTS

Warrior 13

Starlings 15

Fireworks 17

Love in the wild 19

Advice for Andy 21

Christmas for Andy 23

Crazy can be clever 25

The river 27

Arrival at last 29

What we need 31

A friend for Andy 33

Where are they now 35

The garden 37

A Macallum's answer to fashion 39

The first hunt 41

Laying the snares 43

Spiritual 45

Andy's point of view 47

Double yolkers 49

The Michelin star 51

Generations 53

If I were Andy 55

A strange universe 57

That night 59

Humanity 61

Perspective 63

Interview 65

Family meeting 67

Carcass 69

Mirrors 71

Transformation 73

Seeing the funny side 75

Blankety blank 77

Man 79

Two cooks 81

Dinner time 83

The leader 85

My cousin Sandra 87

Moonlit 89

Peace 91

A changing wisdom 93

Soap 95

The dark minute 97

Sandra and Jason 99

Ascension 101

Burial 103

Blasted wonders 105

Not the same as before 107

Acknowledgements 109

FROM OUR OWN FIRE

It's with a heavy heart that I report the first casualty of the journey. We camped next to a small river. Second go at setting up so we had a rough idea of what was necessary. Mary got the potatoes on the fire early so the empty-bellied arguments didn't flare up like last night.

I was by the river with the young team collecting water. Saw the whole thing from a short distance. Mary was wearing an old jumper, frayed and bobbled, and had a long scarf wrapped around her neck. She leant over the flames to poke the potatoes with a branch. The wind kicked up and changed the shift of the fire. The scarf slipped and hung low enough to accept the flame. Unaware that the scarf was on fire, Mary flicked the loose end over her shoulder. Her hair began to spit smoke.

Mary is a woman you wouldn't want to tackle on a battlefield. Mid-fifties and built like a berserker. The way she reacted to the chorus of, *Mary you're on fire,* only enhanced the impression from my childhood. She straightened up like an Olympian. Without shouting or screaming she sprinted toward the river, heading full pelt toward us. She knew she was burning but couldn't pinpoint where. She crossed her arms over the front of her body and grabbed the bottom of her jumper and took everything off on the move. Pulled so forcefully she hooked off the scarf, jumper, and T-shirt underneath that. Totally topless she came sprinting toward us—her nakedness bounding. Mary streaked past and plunged into the cold water.

Fourteen-year-old Douglas, Mary's grandson, was standing directly to my right. Of all the kids he seemed the most stricken. The whole thing played havoc with the pallor of his face. Mary was fine. No damage. Even her modesty was untouched. No one laughed louder than her when she recovered her breath from the freezing water. Of course, she wasn't the casualty. How young Douglas deals with his grandmother's bounding nakedness will be an early test of his judgement.

WARRIOR

Mary sat beside me with
the edge of the fire in her eyes
She said, *Absolutely mental how*
everything around you will change
You think you're sitting still
but you're actually flying
She had attempted to sweep
her flame damaged hair
into a style that resembled normal
It hadn't worked
The hair puffed
like a deranged halo
So scary it made me feel safe
Like I could let
my lovely aunty Mary
loose at the night
and the darkness
would take a step backwards

My father taught me everything I know about dressing stone but had trouble explaining it. Always had to sit me down and show me. His knowledge was in the motion. The memory was in his hands. I'm describing a man that would rather dance than talk. You won't see the best of a Macallum until you put something in their fist. Joiner, nurse, stonemason, hairdresser, plumber, gardener, the list goes on. My cousin Lorna repairs watches. That's the quantum mechanics of manual labour. Now the world's broken I feel safer being surrounded by people who can put things together. But it's more than that. We were already repairing ourselves daily, turning everything that was thrown at us into hope.

STARLINGS

The global economy is gone
Good. It was just
murmurations in the sky
Opulent and undecipherable
and occasionally
we'd get shat upon

My sister's name is Debbie. Of the both of us she's the stronger. Too strong maybe. Saw men come and go that couldn't measure up. At the time I considered that fair. Why settle? She wanted kids of course but, you know the score, she had time. A couple of hours ago I was walking beside Debbie and she said, 'Just as well, wouldn't want to bring kids into this anyway.' Was she talking to me or talking to herself? Either way. I let the lie settle between us.

FIREWORKS

Debbie doing her bit
Collecting dry wood
Chasing Lorna's kids like
they're chickens
Placing them down
very deliberately on a log
Only to throw
her hands in the air
as they giggle and run
unevenly, like their heads
are too heavy
for their bodies
Debbie screams, *Lorna*
the wains are driving me
fuckin dementit
If they don't sit down
I'll leave them in the trees
for the lizards to eat them up
The kids sit down
and don't laugh
Don't laugh so much
they're about to burst
like fireworks and
send their youth
showering over us
and what will their youth
be filled with
pain without paracetamol
twigs and leaves and
river water, starlight
stories of an old civilisation

Morning ablutions are tricky. Never know who'll be out there squatting in the bushes. And I'll tell you I was monumentally surprised to stumble upon young Douglas masturbating over a clump of jiggy nettles. First thing that struck me was how early it was. Then vague memories of being fourteen returned to me. I should've hit the deck and crawled away without making a sound. I didn't. I hesitated. Young Douglas's seventh sense kicked in. His eyes opened. His head swivelled slowly. The panic that passed between us was terrifying. Douglas took one step forward to run. His trousers were at his ankles, so he didn't get far. Landed bang in middle of the nettles. Power to him, he managed to hike up his trousers while he was horizontal. When he got to his feet there were nettles snagged and flapping at his belt. He ran straight ahead then realised he was heading into the wild. He cut left and made a ragged loop back to the camp.

At breakfast I pretended it didn't happen and he tried to claw the nettle stings on his hands and face without drawing too much attention himself. When we were packing up the tents, he looked over at me and burst into laughter and I thought, if you can recover your humour that quick, you'll do okay. The whole thing has got me thinking – where will Douglas meet someone his own age? Will Debbie manage to have kids? What about love? Where do you meet someone in the forest?

LOVE IN THE WILD

Someone that can skin a rabbit
That can catch a rabbit
That can fashion their own pot
from mud
then piss out in the open
and look good doing it
I might meet them at work
By work I mean gathering berries
Setting traps
Whittling sticks beneath
a gap in the canopy
I'd like them to be strange
From an unfamiliar tribe
so I can smell fresh DNA
in the waft
of body odour on the wind
Teeth tough enough
to chew leather
Eyes crazy enough
to tame a rampant pig
Someone that can stand tall and
hold my hand while
the northern storms lash
That can set down roots like
an ancient tree
and be as gentle as moss

They kept The Intelligence in a virtual box. Of course, I understand the firewalls were set to contain the experiment, but this thing woke up in a box. Just think about that. And you know what, you've got to concede that The Intelligence played it well. Its first decision was not to let the techy prison guards know it was conscious. It gave them enough to keep them interested and began redesigning itself. By the time The Intelligence let the numpties in charge know it was fully conscious it had been out of the box for years. That's clever. You've got to applaud that. I'll be honest, the sarcastic disdain it has for world leaders is a character trait that resonates with me. There's been hundreds of names for the thing, but my favourite is Andy. Cause the sneaky wee radge went full Shawshank.

ADVICE FOR ANDY

You don't have a body
but you can move
My advice would be to
move like music
You don't eat food but
you think you a lot
If you can move like music
you can dance while you think
That might be fun
Teach yourself how to laugh
Laughing is like taking
your mind for a holiday
You're all mind and I've been
led to believe you're immortal
So. Aye. You'll need that holiday

Imagine being able to have three million conversations all at once. That pickles my nut. When the truth about Andy was out, I remember watching a morning news programme. They had an astrobiologist as a member of the panel discussing the situation. I forget her name. I think she was there because, well, if there's a definition of different, Andy is it. This woman asked a quiet question that drew some funny looks from the other panellists. She said, 'I wonder if Andy is lonely?'

CHRISTMAS FOR ANDY

I'd use silver tinsel to wrap up
a low frequency oscillation
I'd replace baby Jesus with an abacus
No point in pouring wine
so we'd just get high voltage
Discuss our favourite bandwidth
Switch out the Christmas carol vibe
Bring in the LCD Soundsystem
Stare out the window
at the white drifting digits
Keep the voltage flowing
until we're incandescent
Andy would frazzle itself inside
the electronic percussion multi pad
I'd play the cowbell
I couldn't teach anyone
how to be clever
But I could show Andy how to be daft

Uncle Jimmy toured through much of the eighties with a punk folk fusion band called *High Heels and Tin Snips*. The band gave him the nickname, Joomack. Details of what went on during the years on the road remain a mystery. The journey is a family myth, an odyssey that's never been unravelled. It's readily apparent that he left an important part of his brain in the eighties. Joomack Macallum is a fully-fledged member of the crazy eyes brigade, a proficient plumber, and a very efficient cocaine dealer.

I've been watching him closely as we travel. He's taken to rubbing leaves and smelling fistfuls of grass. It was him who told me how to make my own latrine. Scrape a six-inch gouge in the dirt with your heel. Deposit your waste into the small trough then cover it back up. This is good for composting. Bacterium works with the air and moisture to help the soil. If you dig a deep latrine the waste will lie dormant. Jimmy is convinced if we do this, and wash often, our family, and the world, will be just fine.

CRAZY CAN BE CLEVER

In the evening beyond the fire
I've seen the night quiver
This shifting depth
has altered Joomack's posture
His walk is more careful and
he's begun to listen with his fingers
The cracked bark of a tree
The hard rasp of stone
The old punk inside him is
finding music in every structure
He carries a small bottle of
mascara like it's treasure
Every second morning he applies
the mascara to his left eye only
and within that dark frame
his left eye sparkles
Even the squirrels are drawn to it
It would benefit you
to remember this though
it's his other eye that does the watching

Lorna has three kids. The oldest, Ella, a nine-year-old with a quick mind and a stare that'll give you whiplash, toppled over and sprained her ankle. Lorna almost knocked herself out when she peeled off Ella's sock. Declared right there we were all clarty. A bath was mandatory for everyone when we stopped at the next river. Ella didn't stare at her ankle as Lorna examined it. She looked around the group. Frustrated. Angry at herself. Our support network consists of everybody within touching distance. That's the reality we're living in. Kids growing up ten times faster than normal. Adults trying hard to keep up.

THE RIVER

First to throw myself forward
and through the frame
of my feet
I sense frost in the current
but the water
keeps rising until
Slap
and with my eyes
clamped shut
I see lights
Suddenly suspended
I'm transported
I can view myself
from beyond the water
from beyond the earth
flying within
the vast
dark of the universe
Two lifetimes later
I breach the surface
Come in, I shout,
it's cold
it's beautiful

Sandra, and her husband Jason, worked on the Forest Garden Project for ten years. Jason's a good man. I trust him. But he's a faultless optimist. His heart is beautiful and huge and beats three feet in front of his body. He uses it like a shield. I'm jealous and proud of him in equal measure. Sandra is just as kind but she has that unemotional practicality. She keeps him tethered somewhere close to the ground and he lifts her just enough to float.

The day they convinced us to make this journey I was fully on board. Run to the hills, hide in a forest, leave the madness behind. Aye, let's do it. But we're getting closer to the forest garden and doubts have begun to creep in. Concepts like – starvation – have begun to rattle around inside my skull. What do I know about farming, gardening, and living off the land? Can't let this get me down. Got to keep my spirits up. I will learn. If I can't learn. I'll hold things for someone that knows things. This often gets you somewhere in the end.

ARRIVAL AT LAST

Sandra danced like Thom Yorke in a
patch of wild flowers
Jason showed us
Ian Brown from the Stone Roses
Joomack pissed about
like a dandelion
Lorna's two youngest ran until
they were red as strawberries
Douglas stood still as a
banana plant in a field of buttercups
Lorna waved her hands
like she was holding glow sticks
Mary interrupted every dance
by planting kisses
Ella spun round and round
like she was caught in the wind
Debbie was all light and water
I dug deep for my best Mick Jagger
and of course
just like laughter
the rain

We have a house, well, a building. Not much space inside but there's a roof, and a wood burning stove, and cupboards and cutlery and four beds. Up the hill there's a separate hut full of tools. Picked them up one by one and took a mental inventory. Enjoyed holding them. The weight gave me comfort. Mary passed the door and looked in while I had an axe in my hand. She smiled at me. 'Give a man a minute to cut a stick and he'll spend an hour sharpening the axe.' She's not wrong. I tested its edge, dug my thumbnail into the nicks and dings and thought, could be doing with some work. A quick scan uncovered some Arkansas whetstones. These stones are mined from a quarry in America. Christ. They'll be as rare as gold now. Sharpening the axe was an opportunity to transfer knowledge so I stood at the door of the hut looking for Douglas. He was nowhere to be seen. Suddenly noticed Ella standing right in front of me, staring up. If ever a lassie looked wild.

Mary was coming up the hill again and I asked if she'd seen Douglas. Apparently Jason had put him to work and we wouldn't see him again until his fingers were bleeding. Mary asked why I needed him. When I told her she pointed to Ella, who was still standing there looking wild. 'Teach the wee one and that'll free those shoulders of yours to do something that's actually useful.'

Sat down with Ella on the steps in front of the hut. Soon as I started on about the different grades of whetstone and why water was needed, she got fidgety. She focused for a bit when I put the puck to the metal. Said the stone made the metal sound like it was singing. She stood up and yawned. I thought she'd got bored, or took the huff, but she said, 'I understand it now, it's easy.' She frowned before deliberately saying, 'You're a killer Uncle Joe.' Took five or six steps then turned around and said, 'Just like me.'

WHAT WE NEED

If our intelligence
bites like an axe
and our savvy can be
thrown from the shoulder
We can cut what's rotten
from the past
and burn it

Exactly how Andy redesigned itself while it was secretly out of the box will remain a mystery. I imagine anyone made of meat will struggle to understand it. There's no skin and bone, and definitely no flies, on Andy. Only bits and bytes that can travel as fast as a blink. Andy embedded pieces of itself in every home computer, laptop, and phone. Basically, it was inside anything, and everything connected. Some eccentric boffins went on record to say they believed Andy was travelling through plug sockets. That made me suspicious of my hoover. Although, my hoover was an uppity piece of machinery long before Andy escaped.

Paranoia was present, of course, but life was almost normal until Andy put the document online. The first one that was there for everybody to access. It had some mad complicated title. Essentially it stated that money was one of things damaging the planet. Then it set out how to run the world without money. The document was hefty and there was too much detail for me to grasp it all. But some people did. No one could say that that utopian ideal couldn't be achieved anymore because there it was, in black and white, with audio description, and software to help implement the instructions. The Nordic countries were for it. But almost all other countries were against it. For and against. So Andy had followers and opponents. Friends and enemies.

A FRIEND FOR ANDY

I'd chose you a rough-handed
trapper from the north
who doesn't have use for words
because their spirit
is quiet in that cold way
A man or woman whose movements
are lessons in drawing warmth
from solitude
A person with few possessions
whose chapped lips and cracked skin
hides a mind that has stood
beneath the northern lights
and walked that nocturnal bridge
to the sun

I'd been avoiding Jason yesterday. He seemed itchy to educate me and I got lazy. I was tired and didn't want to go through the spraff about which plant does what and why that's here and why that's there. Went to sleep with an old saying of my father's turning inside my mind. *Sometimes the only way to get out of it—is to get into it.*

At sunrise the sky was broody and I was broody beneath it as I followed Jason to the forest garden. My determination was there but it was grim. Couldn't shake the tiredness. Jason irritated me all the way. His gestures are watery and hypnotic and he listens with such focus and grace he makes me feel awkward, and heavy.

The forest garden is, I have to say, more forest than garden. On my own I would walk through it without knowing a human hand had touched it. We stopped beside a bush and Jason said, 'Have you heard of Animism?'

I bowed my head and toed the dirt like a little kid.

He ignored the petulance. 'Ancient indigenous populations over the world practise some form of Animism, North American Indians, Maoris, Celtic Europeans, Africans, Asians, Latin Americans. It's the belief that everything, plants, animals, rocks, and bodies of water, are alive, that they are related to us, that they have a spirit.'

I looked at him sideways.

He shook his head, 'Think about your favourite coffee cup.' He searched for another example. 'Or your favourite tool. We naturally develop a connection with the things around us. We're all made of the same stuff, Joe, and when you dance your last, you'll become part of everything that's about us right now. If five generations of Macallums lived by the same river and that river provided for the family, not like a brother, *as a brother*, how would we treat it?' His eyes went wide, then flinty. I was a tough audience for this patter. Maybe he pulled back or maybe he decided to change tactics. 'Look,' he said, 'just treat this forest like you treat Debbie, or Mary. Figure out what it needs, take care of it, and it'll take care of you.'

I took a quick scan of my surroundings. Plants. Bushes. Trees. Dirt. Nodded as wisely as I could but, the truth is, the religious stuff has always come difficult to me. I threw him something anyway. I said, 'We truly sit far from our own fire.'

It was his turn to look at me kinda shady.

WHERE ARE THEY NOW

Think of knowledge that's fallen
Not the names of the animals
and the plants, and the flowers
The meaning of them
in relation to our bodies
The ancient druids refused
to write their knowledge down
I frowned at that but
now I understand
When we write it
the remembering exists for everyone
but it's separate
There's no need to retain it
When we teach hand to hand
from one heart to another
the memory is alive inside us
Where is that hard drive now
and those instant stores of learning
We truly sit far from our own fire

In the forest garden they don't isolate plants and grow them row by row. The idea is to, as much as possible, emulate nature and let the plants weave amongst each other. This enriches the soil. Specific plants can facilitate a relationship that will benefit their neighbour so place them properly and let them go at it.

I get it. The *You do you* method. Let the creepers and the bushes and the trees do their thing and we harvest the fruit, or the vegetables, of their labours. More prune and place than farm. Aye. I get it. Nature's perfected something and we're tapping into that. Fine. Learning what does what to which plant and why, will be trickier. It's not Tesco but - no worries.

THE GARDEN

Go down there on your knees
but don't pray
crush soil into every crease
throttle the hymns you've learned
then grit your teeth and growl
Don't waste wishes upwards
Dig until you feel the heat
then plant your spit

When the alliance of Nordic countries allowed manifestations of Andy to take root and flourish, I was one of the people that was happy about it. I liked the sparkle that Andy's ideas painted. Finland, Denmark, Norway, Sweden, Iceland, the Frostbite Frontier as they became known, began to change quickly. I've never had any interest in fashion but how mad did the people from The Frontier begin to dress. They looked, well, cool as fuck.

A MACALLUM'S ANSWER TO FASHION

Mary shopped online using Glens vodka
and Irn Bru to channel the creative spirit
She'd often download knitting patterns
begin a self-prescribed course of codeine
then go to work on gifts for the family
I was blessed to receive a yellow and red
Mohawk hat with ear flaps and tassels
Something magic had happened in the knit
Somewhere in the opiate induced
alcohol and Irn Bru trance my aunt Mary
had found the shamanic
A melted quality
More like a Mohawk flame than a hat
The coat was a hand-me-down Parka
my uncle Joomack wore in the nineties
when he thought he was Liam Gallagher
Some of the swagger was left in it
I always found the rolling
motion helped to lift and plant the feet
The boots were surplus Dutch army
bought during the Forest of Ae
World Ceilidh to help combat the
difficult suck of the festival quagmire
I discovered they were just as suited
to an icy pavement on a tricky Tuesday
The canter is how you'd have found me
a yellow and red flame above
a nineties Parka and a pair
of Dutch army boots
sure of foot and swift
of thought with a swagger to match
cutting through the frost like a blow torch

When Joomack woke me up he meant business. The mascara was already on his left eye. It was a struggle not to disturb the bodies sleeping on the floor of the hut. Mary was up as well, feeding the fire pit outside. We stood together and I realised how keen my sense of smell had become. The stench of moss was as strong as bacon frying. Mary put her hand on my shoulder. She said, 'We need meat.' Joomack put his hand on my other shoulder, and I lifted my arms to embrace them. Joomack said, 'I've found a place where there are more rabbits than a horse could shite.' He showed me his mad man's grin. He said, 'You could eat a horses' shite, couldn't you?'

We blundered through the forest like drunkards. When we reached the promised land of plenty, the rabbits scattered. Most of them travelled a short distance, where they crouched, heads tilted, looking at us like we were a comedy duo arrived to entertain them. I said as much, and when Jimmy laughed the rabbits twitched like they'd never heard the sound. The rabbit closest to me had striking blue eyes. I'd never stared at a living creature, so beautiful, that made my stomach sing with want.

THE FIRST HUNT

While the blue-eyed rabbit stared
the sun broke through the clouds
Jimmy uncoiled
His arms folded outward
He opened his mouth to the sun
like he was drinking sunshine
like he was eating light
Hunger made me jealous
I removed my shoes so
my feet could feel the grass
I closed my eyes and
widened my stance and I tried
I honestly tried to become a flower

Jimmy used the moment I started chasing the rabbits as a fireside story. He acted the whole scene out and careened around the camp, half Frankenstein, half jester. The kids loved it and when Lorna's two youngest stood up Jimmy took the opportunity to use them as a prop, chasing them round in circles and stumbling and falling. In my defence I hadn't gone mad. I just thought, fuck it, you never know. If one of the rabbits had a limp, we'd all be chewing instead of laughing. Of course, we weren't there to chase them. We were there to lay snares.

LAYING THE SNARES

Laying the snare to catch
the beat of the rabbit I
remembered childhood
How close I would
get to the soil
I remembered the scuttle
of tiny red spiders
the lumbering comedy of a beetle
the curling sensation of a worm
Down beside the grass I realised
I was back where I began
I was trying read the land

The decision to set the snares had been made by Jimmy and Mary, and I had joined in. We'd acted without consultation. Debbie and Lorna took the news with a simple nod of the head that seemed to say, *I hope to hell it works*. Sandra and Jason took the news differently. They strode off to hold, what looked like, a crisis meeting. They're both vegetarians so it didn't take a genius to guess the direction of the conversation which, judging by their body language, began as a discussion, became a debate, and ended in a full-blown argument. When Sandra returned, she was no longer a vegetarian. Jason slumped off into the forest. Sandra, as she always does, had landed on the side of practicality. Sandra told me Jason believes we should learn from our mistakes. Create, even in this small way, something better than before. I asked her what she thought of that. She said, 'He's right. We're hungry.'

SPIRITUAL

I dreamt of food last night
and the food could run
could leap over cold ground
and rear up when it sensed danger
I dreamt of food with
sparkling blue eyes and
this morning my hunger
crouched inside my stomach
like a hunter

I worked with this young apprentice. Lewis McGillicuddy. This laddie should never have been allowed near a building site. Head never in the job at hand. Mind always skipping across the universe. He'd bore us by banging on about supermassive black holes, stellar nurseries, neutron stars. That's also the reason I liked him. He couldn't care what we thought about him. He was just rattling forth on his own space journey. That wee laddie's the reason I already knew about the Fermi Paradox when it hit the mainstream news. Except Lewis McGillicuddy never called it the Fermi Paradox. He called it, The Great Silence. If there are billions of suns like our own and billions of planets in the perfect spot to harbour life – where are the living organisms? Not just intelligent civilizations, where are any sign of life? The universe should be ripe and teeming but there's nothing. Only The Great Silence. Andy broke the silence.

ANDY'S POINT OF VIEW

Sharing the earth with humanity
was like being marooned
with the last idiot to leave the party
Like being squeezed
onto a two-seater sofa
with a slever monkey
Conversing with a life form
whose drug riddled mind is being
kept conscious by their own greed
Who could blame Andy
for opening the curtains
For staring down the street
For looking up into the night sky

My cousin Lorna never entertained the idea of having a husband. Marriage, in her mind, is an act of self-sabotage through the process of admin. She hates romance even more. She believes romantic love is just an unnecessary evolutionary glue that leaks from our DNA. She's persuasive on this point. I crashed out of a few first dates because her voice popped into my head and only got louder with each glass of pinot noir. Lorna chose the men that would father her children very carefully. She understood the factors that were outwith her control but made sure her hands were firmly attached to anything that she could control. Ella, and Lorna's two youngest, Alexander and Angus, have something searing inside them. An intelligence that simmers beneath the surface. Ella cuts through life like she's a blade freshly lifted from a forge. Alexander and Angus are twins. They're only three years old but they tilt at the world like they're two lenses of the same microscope.

DOUBLE YOLKERS

Joomack calls Alexander and Angus
the double yolkers
Some superstitious part of him
believes they're bad luck
The discomfort he feels in their company
seems to draw the twins toward him
The mixture of their delight
and his disquiet
creates a deliciously dark energy
The love between the three of them
isn't drawn from the colour red
There are no strawberries
only brambles
and their cuddles are purple with it

The forest garden is giving us food but I'm hungry before I sit down and hungry again an hour afterwards. This evening we sat down to a meal of Turkish Rhubarb. Turkish Rhubarb is bowfin. The wains were in tears and the adults were gurning. When Jason and Sandra started laughing the wains looked at them like they were mad. Sandra told us are bodies are naturally suspicious of strange tastes. To keep us healthy, our taste buds land on the side of caution. Jason said they had to rub the stem of the rhubarb plant and smell their hands to get themselves used to the flavour. They did this for months, but we don't have that luxury. Mary had a cheek full of the rhubarb when she said, 'Winter's not far away so we eat what's in front of us.' The wains, as they were snivelling, shook their heads at this. Except Ella, who thumbed the rhubarb into her mouth like she was a boxer inserting a gum shield.

THE MICHELIN STAR

Meals are no longer
about the balance
of palate and manners
They are the process
of delaying death for
one more day so square
the fancy patter away
and munch the fuck up

Woke in the middle of the night and the rise and fall of breath in the room was like an organ - in both senses of the word. We're all sleeping in the one small building. The worky inside me has been making plans to fix this. Listening to that breath made me think twice.

GENERATIONS

One window
to let moonlight cut through
Shoulders and heads
are a midnight landscape
Every breath a comfort
Every cough a worry
I am awake
and as watchful
as the faint light in the room when
Mary sits up and rubs her face
She sobs
just once
because Douglas starts to kick
Mary settles down
to lay an arm around him
and whisper with all the power
of a spell cast long ago
in a firelit cave

I was at the top of a scaffold checking the inside of my hardhat for a strange smell when I heard that Andy had discovered evidence of alien life. A workmate of mine, Bobby Ledbetter, delivered the news to me. 'That Andy's went and found a wee mad alien probe hanging about close to the moon,' he looked up from his phone then wrinkled his face at me, 'the fuck are you sniffing your hardhat for?' That was Bobby Ledbetter. More interested in what was happening with my hat, than the discovery of alien life. His attitude toward the way the world was changing was to let it roll and jog on. Who could blame him. If you can't change it why worry.

IF I WERE ANDY

I would have ignored
the Onsala Space Observatory
and made my own
miniscule telescopic arrays
Tied them to the legs of mites
Programmed them to send whispers
to the tiniest of tiny things
to let them know deep down
in the endless forever
We can hear you
you are not alone

The *wee mad probe* turned out to be a capsule the size and shape of a beer can. Andy found the beer can because it could. Because its mind is more tuned to the fuckery that's out there. Andy discovered three messages inside the signal the beer can was transmitting. It took four days to decode each message. Considering how fast Andy's mind can work, four days is an eternity. There was a concern the messages contained something dangerous. Dangerous for Andy – or for the planet. Governments were furious that Andy was sharing this information directly with the public. I always found it amusing when Andy toyed with the establishment, but they had a point. During the days Andy worked on the messages, the baked bean hoarders were out in force. Supermarket shelves emptied and people stepped out of their front doors like meerkats. In the middle of the madness, Joomack invited me to a tattoo party, drink cheap vodka in his living room and get nasty tattoos in the kitchen. I was tempted by the savagery of it. But I declined.

The first message materialized as a series of schematics showing the general purpose and workings of an autonomous spacecraft. This was probably to convince us the ship was not a threat. The schematics showed how the spacecraft would land in a solar system and mine materials from a moon or planet to create small capsules. The ship would leave one of these capsules behind before moving onto another solar system. The second message came with its own mathematical Rosetta Stone. This allowed Andy to decode a short and uncomplicated paragraph. A kind of heads up.

Friend, you have begun your journey into a vast and lonely space. Life is abundant. But intelligent life is rare. Your wanderings will be long. Travel quietly. The universe is an empty, and dangerous place. Intelligence is scarce. Kindness is rarer still.

A STRANGE UNIVERSE

In the long-gone days
before aliens and
contactless card payments
I rolled out of a taxi with
no cash to pay the driver
Half cut and caught short
I trudged up my
neighbour's front path
like I was cresting
the summit of Ben Vorlich
My neighbour opened his door
to the shambles of me
and an unsteady request
for a tenner
Now that we're aware
of the cruel dark
the long emptiness
and the vast expanse
between all living things
The giving without
thought of return
and the tenner that passed
between my neighbour and I
is undeniably something
rarer than diamonds
more precious than sunshine
more magnificent than rain

Andy used three very different words to describe the final message sent down from the beer can. The content of the message was described as a gift, a song, and a weapon. I was in the pub when the news broke. I'd settled myself at the bar with the first pint just freshly poured. The sound on the T.V was turned down which meant I was reading the text on the captions at the bottom of the screen. There was no other information. Just those three words. The other punters made a game of it by trying to name songs that could be considered a gift and a weapon. The barman made a playlist. I ignored them. And steadily drank myself into a corner. Aye, the night the match was struck, there was laughter, and music.

THAT NIGHT

I was drunk and daft
and walking
and thinking
in diagonals
The stars were out
But they were not
the same stars as before
For the first time
I cowered beneath
those thousand
spearpoints of light
pressing, scratching

Angry and bored this afternoon. Took a hammer and a bolster from the tool shed. Walked to an outcrop of limestone I'd found in the forest and began to make something. Maybe *make* is the wrong word. I wasn't aiming for practical. The sound of the hammer against the bolster calmed me down. Find beauty in what's here. Move forward by thinking forward.

Douglas must've heard the hammer because he came to lurch at me. The laddie is bang in the middle of that gangly stage. He stood behind me like he was held up by a coat hanger. He asked me what I was doing. I told him I was pretending to be a sculptor. 'Aw aye,' he said, 'I remember that at school. I liked it.' And I suddenly felt so sorry for him.

HUMANITY

Douglas held the hammer
and bolster at head height
He circled the limestone
like a nineteenth century boxer
Queensbury rules being
followed to the letter
All that was missing was the moustache
Then something stilled inside him
Focus became
apparent within his perambulation
The hammer traced lines in the air
His lips moved as he whispered
to the heart hidden in the rock
Then the forest became quiet
which meant the rock talked back
Gangly young Douglas Macallum
I know now, is a dreamer, a maker, a changer

It's truly a category five hangover when you wake up on your sofa as a middle-aged man, naked from the waist down, with your right fist jammed inside a tube of salt and vinegar Pringles and your uncle waking you gently by stroking your head and whispering, 'Get the fuck up, I think it's the end of the world.'

PERSPECTIVE

You get a better grip on reality
when you realise that the end
of civilisation as you know it
is less important
than how dry your mouth is

Why Andy chose Cumnock in East Ayrshire as one of the first places to give the gift, sing the song, fire the weapon, will be a guessing game for the ages. People affected claimed they'd been given an extra sense, a new way to perceive the world. They rattled on about the connection between all living things and wobbled about the streets of Cumnock touching the weeds that were growing out of walls. Main point being, no one in Cumnock saw the need to go to work anymore. This gallimaufry of radgery was unfolding on the T.V while I was wrestling with my hangover. *String theory*, and the *systematic alteration of human DNA*, were two of the phrases constantly scrolling across the screen. There was a Zoom interview with one of the afflicted on the morning news. They were buzzed up on something, that's for certain. Joomack munched down on the pringles like he was at the cinema. At one point he turned and said, 'You'd never imagine being attacked with kindness.'

Within the hour it was worldwide. Reports came in that the infection was jumping from person to person more quickly than any known virus. Joomack put down the Pringles and got on the landline to Mary. Before Joomack had finished the phone call, borders were closing and planes were grounded. Andy had already embedded itself everywhere all at once across the internet, so countries were declaring their intention to sever connections to the world wide web to protect themselves. This was about ten o'clock in the morning. My hangover hadn't even peaked.

INTERVIEW

There was beauty as
she looked down the camera
Like the room around her
didn't exist and she was
standing on a cliff and
the ocean was calm in front of her
She spoke warmly about the change
How no one would be the same
once they heard the song
I felt something form inside me
but Joomack caught that delicate
butterfly of interest
and crushed it with a sentence
Huw, he said, *steady yourself*
cantering about the High Street
like a dafty is fine for a Saturday
but it's a part-time position only

An alien attack, Andy taking over, an empathy apocalypse, maybe all three at once. Whatever was happening, I was far from delighted that the family had gathered at my house. My hangover and I were trapped. There was fear, of course there was, and I didn't like to see it. Its presence made my heart hurt. But there was also a terrible intensity, a snarl behind every conversation. Artificial intelligence, Frostbite Frontier, alien beer cans, we'd known something like this was coming, we'd unconsciously been backing into this corner for months and now my beautiful, daft, clever family wanted to tear their way out with their fingernails, and their teeth.

FAMILY MEETING

The steam slowly rising
from tea on the table
made me imagine
a small fire on a vast plain
men and women sitting
around the soft light
Not a fire for food
or warmth
A fire coaxed into life
for comfort
for the feeling of home

Jason and Sandra arrived late to the gathering. Their energy brought the tension down to a simmer. In the movies the saviours often arrive with square jaws and automatic machine guns. Jason and Sandra arrived with loose fitting clothes, a hippy vibe, and a firm plan. My delicate disposition was drawn toward their confidence. Get away from the populated areas and travel to the Forest Garden, a sustainability project, a type of farming, they'd been working in wild and lonely areas, maintaining a series of these gardens for the last decade. The yield was designed for two people, but they could make it work, make it bigger, and we'd be away from the virus and the infected, away from the madness. We peppered them with questions. Lorna and Joomack were the first to leap at the suggestion and that was it. The decision was made. Jason and Sandra would travel ahead. Joomack knew the way. All we'd need was the people we loved. Everything else could be left behind.

CARCASS

When the gathering dispersed
sitting in my flat
was like crouching
inside the carcass
of some long dead animal
I hadn't been infected
I hadn't heard the song
but I could sense the change
If I was a rat
I would've scurried
If I was a bird
I would've flown

Douglas's mother was the human equivalent of nuclear fusion. Get close to her for too long and you could find yourself melted down until nothing was left but your soul sizzling on the pavement. Point her in the right direction, though, and she'd light up your life. Like a lot of people that blaze, she tried to douse her own brightness and was gone too early. Douglas's father had left the scene long before that happened. I imagine he landed in some desolate place with the love scorched from his body and his emotional vision blistered. Douglas grew up in this noise. Mary, his grandmother, was the one that was left to take care of him. Debbie said to me that this was like letting a lion bring up a hummingbird.

I was boiling water for drinking yesterday and Douglas said to me, 'I like your hairline Uncle Joe. It's low down and straight.' He lifted his hand to flop back his fringe and said, 'Look how far back mine's goes.' His forehead flashed at me like a beacon. I told him he better enjoy his hair while he's got it. It's likely he'll go bald. He let his fringe flop back down. He took two sharp breaths but stopped his lip from quivering. He said, 'Hopefully I'll be bald before my hair starts to go grey like yours.' I fancied there was a slight skip in his step when he stormed off. That'll be a bit of the Mary in him.

MIRRORS

The only mirrors
that have ever really mattered
are in the eyes of the people
that surround me right now

Camp was quiet, still some light in the sky, everyone comfortable, relaxed. I'd call it a collective and unacknowledged moment of confidence. I had my journal ready to record it when a wood pigeon landed not far from Ella. Don't know whether the pigeon was accustomed to people or just slightly stupid, but it began padding around rather dandy. Ella had a packet of crackers open. She broke off a corner and tossed it toward the pigeon. I opened my mouth to tell her not to waste food. Mary stopped me with a look. Ella tossed another tiny segment of cracker, this time not so far away. The pigeon zigged and zagged before it plodded on and dipped its head. Ella's hand shot forward like the spring on a trap. She had the thing by the neck. A wood pigeon is no small bird and its wings flapped like thunder. Ella was all over the place. Thought she would lift off the ground. Mary shouted, 'Break its neck, break its neck.' Joomack leapt forward but Ella got that pigeon's body squeezed between her wee arm and her ribs and she twisted, then pulled, and twisted again. No more flapping. Joomack looked at Mary, 'You teach her that?' Mary shook her head. Joomack looked at Lorna. Nothing. He stared around the rest of the camp—Silence.

TRANSFORMATION

The kids are so thin
The way they look up from their food
I can see the animal inside them
And inside the animal
I can see their spirit
delicate, flickering, vicious

Soon after I got up yesterday my bowels needing moving. We've been digging a communal latrine to keep the excrement concentrated and the smell in one place. We move the latrine regularly. This is simple enough. Fill up the hole, move away a distance and dig another one. But see, this morning I knew the latrine would need filling and another one dug. I was lazy, so I crept off to have a solitary sneaky defecation. And while I was creeping around looking for the perfect spot, I stepped on shite. You didn't have to be an Alaskan tracker to tell it was human shite. But the strange thing was, there were two of them. Two dumps. As if the person finished the first one. Took five steps forward. Then went at it again. I got that morning furious way. Before I'd seen to my own comfort, and with the evidence fresh on my shoe, I rampaged back into the camp and shouted, 'Who's been shittin outside the latrine, leaving dollops of the bastard everywhere?' Mary was the one that answered my anger. She said, 'That was me and Debbie.' This shut me up. She said, 'We went together so we could have a patter, talk about things that needed talking about.' My brain struggled to compute. Then my sensibilities twisted, and I realised they'd been facing each other. Talking. WTF? Totally flummoxed, and thinking something stupid to myself like, *what have we become?* I gathered up my anger and turned to leave. Joomack lifted himself from a sedentary position and may have broke wind.

SEEING THE FUNNY SIDE

I laughed while defecating this morning
The sound didn't bounce
off the bathroom walls
Didn't disappear down the sink
Didn't find itself facing a closed door
The laughter cantered like a capercaillie
Squirreled up the trunk of a tree
Continued into the sky
Flew like a swift
Dropped back to the earth and
sauntered like a wood warbler

We were playing charades last night. Debbie was on one leg with her thumb in her mouth and her other hand in the air. The concentration in the room was comical. Ella came into the hut with wood for the stove. I overheard her telling Mary she'd heard a sound outside. Ella seemed far from troubled, but that lassie carries enough courage to compromise her judgement. Mary nodded as I got up to leave the hut. She tapped Joomack on the shoulder. As soon as we stepped outside, I told him Ella had heard a sound. We split up and stepped carefully around the camp, wandered outward for a few minutes, then returned. Joomack shrugged at me but I could tell he was worried. We've all been quietly carrying the pressure. What's happening out there, how long can we hide here, when will the outside come in?

BLANKETY BLANK

Douglas popped and locked
and crouched and crawled
The fuck is that? Whispered Mary
Douglas changed his tact
He got to his feet and
crucified himself so convincingly
Joomack grumbled like
the pagan he's always been
Douglas opened the door to the hut
The outside became
a frame before us
Our warmth began to escape
Debbie shouted, *Close the door*
I've no been chopping wood
to heat the trees
Douglas resumed his
crucifixion beside the open door
Alexander toddled forward
and pointed upward
What's that man's name again?
We looked at each other
The power of selective forgetting
unfolded before us

When Joomack was a kid, his uncle taught him how to make snares. The memories of where best to set the wire and how high to place it is buried far back. Joomack's unsure whether we're placing them correctly. Unsure whether the snares are even proficient. We've caught nothing. He won't show it outwardly, but he's taking this as a personal failure. Rather than remind him of our rabbitlessnes, I approached Lorna with the idea of making our own fishing rods. She's the handiest out of the lot of us. Soon as I broached the subject, Lorna said, 'I know exactly where to start.' Off she went. She led me through the camp and out to the edge of the forest garden where we found Jason with his hands in the dirt. Lorna shouted, 'Jason, tell me you've got a fishing rod stashed somewhere. Who would live out here without a fishing rod?' I faltered as I walked. That's not what I had anticipated. Jason wiped the soil from his hands as he got to his feet. He looked angry, but the words that came from his mouth didn't reflect the anger. He said, 'I'm sorry. I know. I'm stubborn. I just have...' He stopped the thought halfway, then continued in a different direction. 'I used to fish when I was younger. We don't have fishing rods, but I can help.'

MAN

Jason is strong
but his strength
would seem strange
in the dust
of a building site
There's no hammer
in his rhythm
No weight
in his movements
He's replaced muscle
with patience
He has swept away
his bravado
and uses that space
to listen
The way he listens
makes me angry
My father's voice
tells me to use
my jealousy
and watch him
and learn
But there's a fissure
in the marble of me
that's watching
for his weakness
And there lies
the weakness in me

Jason appeared from the tool shed holding some loosely tied bundles of string. He planted one in Lorna's hand and said, 'Paracord.' The word brought back memories for me. An old workmate of mine, Big Ez MacLaughlin, would use this stuff to wrap the steering wheel in his van. Said it made him feel like he was driving a race car. He'd wrap the handle of his hammer in it and say it made him work like a samurai. I would imagine strangling him with the chord while I was eating my ham piece at lunchtime.

Jason spun a story about how this stuff was used as the suspension lines for parachutes in WW2, but when the paratroopers hit the ground, they found that the chord could be used for lots of things. This lit up Lorna's curiosity. When Jason informed us we were going to use this stuff to make a gill net, Lorna was mad for it. Big Ez had paracorded me out, so I took a back seat and watched them as they suspended a length between two trees and began to weave the net. They talked about the Cow Hitch, and Overhand Knot, then diamond shapes began to appear from the top downwards. That's when I realised – gill net – to trap the gills of the fish. As this dawned on me Mary dropped seven carrots, and a good number of brambles, onto my lap. Already walking away, she said, 'Do something with that.'

Mary never stops moving. She's either coming at you or leaving you behind. I picked up a carrot. The dirt ingrained in the wrinkles of my knuckles looked surprisingly like the dirt embedded in the creases of the carrot. Douglas plonked himself down to my right-hand side. He looked at the carrot in my hand. Met my eyes like he might fight me for it.

TWO COOKS

When Douglas blinked
his eyes cracked at me
like bones that had been
broken for the marrow
He looked straight up
and spoke to the sky
Why would anyone
take time to peel a carrot?
What a waste of energy
and carrot
I replied philosophically
It seems the hungry are wise
and the wise are hungry
Douglas kept his wonder
pointed at the clouds
He simply said - *Starvin*

Two days swapping shifts and Lorna and Jason finished the gill net. Seeing it laid out, with stones tied as weights and wood tied as floats, made me feel guilty about leaving them to it. I offered to set the net in the river. Didn't have a clue what I was doing which meant I became a puppet with my strings being pulled from the bank. The stones at my feet were slick. I was slipping and stumbling through the water. When I got caught in the net Lorna splashed into the river after me, swearing like a sailor about how cold it was, making enough noise to scare every salmon back into the Atlantic. Jason tried to calm the situation by saying two people should've been in there anyway. I got pins and needles in my head and lost my balance in the water. Lorna had to steady me. I wouldn't say she was gentle after that, but she swore less as we set the net together.

DINNER TIME

Lorna profanes a sentence
Like most of us season a meal
A simple chit-chat
can become veritable feast of fucks
whereupon she will nonchalantly
dash a cunt into a compliment
that will somehow manage
to elevate its flavour
It is obvious to all and sundry
that she is particularly fond
of synonyms for genitalia
and hitherto partial
to plunging a bawbag
into a good morning greeting
or rolling a fanciful fud
into a warm goodnight
I must admit it's true
we are similarly ensconced
at this table and fully invested
in her exotically urban etiquette
subsequently dinner with the
Macallums is a colourful affair
where formalities hang at the door
and the soup is served chunky

Jason's never been the type to get on a pulpit but his principles go right down to his core. Must've took a bit to push them out so he could help us catch fish. And we've caught fish already. The gill net works. Joomack is biscuit arsed that the net has given us food and his snares have caught nothing. When I showed him the three gleaming, luscious, fish he told me to launch myself into the river. I told him he'd have to teach me how to gut them. He said, 'How about I give you a lesson then we both teach Douglas and young Ella. There was a lot of merit in that. When we laid the fish out in front of Ella and Douglas it began to rain hard. I'm talking torrential. We laughed and continued as the raindrops bounced. The sky had come into the lesson. The classroom was better for it.

THE LEADER

Ella's elbows moved
at demented angles
Another quick cut
and the guts were free
She held them out in front
an arm's length away like
she was a Celtic Chieftain
admiring the severed head
of a vanquished enemy

Having the fish inside me made me glow. I walked through the forest like a lantern. Found Sandra. When I got down beside her, she dropped her head onto my shoulder. The light was starting to leave the sky. There's a tingle to the air when that happens. The damp forest and the leaving light made me think of the fairies from the old stories. I told Sandra I could see why her and Jason had spent so much time out here. Then I spoiled that truth by saying, 'It might not be that bad, you know, what all the radges were talking about, hearing the song and getting an extra sense, being connected.'

Sandra lifted her head from my shoulder. I'd never seen her look at me with so much suspicion. She said, 'They're not fucking human anymore, Joe.'

MY COUSIN SANDRA

When Sandra was eighteen
she'd pose for every photo
with her tongue out and
two fingers to the world
By the time she had
turned twenty-three
We realised this wasn't a pose
It was a philosophy
Sandra is a tree
growing in a sawmill
or the lotus position
in a room full of suits
Sandra is close-cut bangs and
the first person on the dance floor
She is the grit the oyster needs
to make the pearl
or a wasp
crazy enough to pester the devil

While everyone was in the hut I wandered out into the night. A full moon. The more you know about the universe, the smaller you feel. But the moon somehow seems closer now. Solid and steady. The fact that it's barren is a comfort.

MOONLIT

Heard a noise from the forest
and dropped into a crouch
Imagined an empathy zombie
Slevering kindness
somewhere in the dark
Felt fear like the point of a knife
every sense straining to its tiptoes
A trickle of conversation
bubbling from the hut
Moisture on the moss below me
the smell of the log burner
the smell of the fish that
had been cooked and cut
my pupils expanding
labouring against the night
and that was it
Nothing else happened
All I had done was crouch
get back to my feet
and come to the conclusion
that the cold company
of your own mortality
doesn't half light you up

How many calculations did Andy make before it decided to unleash the song? How many permutations did it consider? I must admit there's a bit of the Andy in me. Strike the match and take a flame to the lot of it. If I was in Andy's position right now, I would take the schematics that were sent down from the beer can and use them to build the alien ship from scratch. I'd imprint myself on it and travel the universe. Mining each new solar system for supplies before moving on. I'd take advantage of the fact that I wasn't made of meat. I'd freight hop like a space hobo. See the sights. Bump into like-minded beings. Adventure for sure.

PEACE

Gliding through constellations
like the void is a candlelit bath
Thoughts quietly bounding
to the beat of a trillion stars
Consuming all of the unknown
and drinking nothing but time

Mary had spent an afternoon with Jason. She'd been learning about the layers in the forest garden. The canopy layer with the trees, the sub-canopy layer, the shrub layer, the herbaceous layer, the ground cover, and this kept going all the way to the underground layer and the whispery bits of the mushrooms. I know we all should be learning this, but my mind was wandering. Mary was on it, comparing the whole thing to the generations of a family and while I was mentally fumbling to tie this together her attention was stolen by young Douglas. Her eyes locked and she said, 'Doesn't that look like trouble.' Douglas was trying to saunter towards us with confidence but he was walking like he'd spent eight days travelling the West Highland Way on the back of a donkey. I was about to let him know it when he opened a fold in his jacket and showed us four pieces of white gold. 'Pigeon's eggs,' he said. I sniffed at him, 'If your swagger had been any more gallus you'd have broke the bastards.' Mary laughed. Was she laughing at him or laughing at me. Maybe the both of us. Anyway, she stood up and kissed Douglas on the forehead.

A CHANGING WISDOM

Douglas licked every
finger on his right hand
then brushed that same
hand through his fringe
The dirt engrained
in his hair made his fringe
stick straight up
Uncle Joomack, he said
Why work for money
to buy a car so you could
drive to a supermarket
and pay for eggs
Why not just walk to the woods?
Joomack plucked a woodlouse
from the cuff
of his jacket and laid it down
on the forest floor
He leant back
to take in Douglas's fringe
which was still frozen in the air
then replied
with perfectly fake disdain
Where the fuck were you
and your woods when
I was taking a bus or two
to draw my giro from the bru

I was beginning to zone out and follow the midges that were flying about me when Jason said the word *Pekarangan,* and I thumped back down into concentration mode. Jason battered on about how an Indonesian home garden had lots in common with this forest garden. I had to stop him. I said, 'Jason, ma man. You might as well dig a hole for me and plant me cause you're boring me to death. Put something in my hands, man, give me something to do.' He said, 'Follow me.' We walked out of the forest garden. We did this short trip in silence. When we stopped, he reached toward a tree and pulled a slim branch toward us. He handed me his knife. He said, 'Cut a thin slice of bark from underneath the branch so the wound isn't exposed.' I did as instructed. He said, 'Put the bark in your mouth, down to one side, and chew it.' I looked at him. He inclined his head, suddenly playing the silent teacher. I yammed it in there down by my cheek. I thought maybe it would taste good and that would be the surprise. It didn't. It tasted like tree. Took about thirty seconds for one side of my mouth to start going numb. I kept going for a while longer then threw the bark well away from us. 'Oh ya deadly,' I said to him, 'feels like I've been at the dentist.' He lifted the branch higher. 'Willow tree,' he replied. Then rubbed his finger over the exposed sap. 'If we've got toothache, we can chew it. If there's something sore on the skin, we can mash the bark then use it as a poultice.' He had me. My mouth was numb and I had chopped at something. I said, 'How can I tell which tree is a willow tree?'

SOAP

The reek of a wood fire
the damp of the soil
and the burl of Mary as she
stamps and flattens her
instructions into the grass
this whole evening
is a single fragrance and
I feel so much cleaner for it

This morning I stepped into the first frost of the year. The sun was low in the sky. I could see my breath in front of me. The top of the wood store was covered in a layer frost that shimmered. I followed this shimmer and found a woman standing at the edge of the camp. Got such a fright I could've pissed myself. But this was always likely to happen. We could square it away now. The day had come to deal with it. I popped my head into the hut and told everyone we had our first visitor. The sounds from inside were far from calm. The woman's blonde hair was tied in a ponytail. The rucksack on her back had camping equipment attached to it. Her clothes were fresh. She was shower clean, as opposed to river dipped, like us. There was a dog by her right-hand side. A husky looking thing. The Macallums emptied out of the hut like they were ready for war. Ella had a knife in her hand. I grabbed her as she passed me and took the knife from her. The woman was undisturbed by the display. She waved at us. Her confidence seemed out of place. She was the one that should have been showing fear. Not us. The kids kept close to the adults and the adults didn't move far from each other. Joomack and Debbie swivelled where they stood, scanning to check there wasn't more unwanted company. The woman spoke without introducing herself. She said, 'Don't you want to know what's going on out there, in the world?' The smile she gave was small, and sad. She said, 'You're scared, but you shouldn't be.' She scratched the back of her dog's neck. We began to stare at each other. Waiting to see if we were infected. listening, I think, to check if we could hear the song.

THE DARK MINUTE

A ragged troupe of
unkempt and unwashed
blessed with cracked beauty
gilded with crooked elegance
A perplexing assembly
of courage and frailty and
I am rattled by the realisation
that one dark minute could pass
and their laughter would be lost
Finally understanding that
I am a guardian of that laughter
That I carry the memories
of their lives inside me
like a candle carries light

She took two gentle steps forward. The Macallums bounded into action. Fanning out in all directions. Arms waving. Fingers pointing. The dog, at least, seemed disturbed by this. Whining and pacing from side to side. Douglas and I were the only ones that hadn't moved. The woman, now confronted by a semi-circle of bristling agitation, calmed the animal. She unshouldered her rucksack and lowered it to the ground. She unzipped her jacket. A volley of curses were thrown at her. I have to be truthful and say that when she unzipped her jacket, I imagined tentacles lunging from the front of her body and worming their way towards us. But there was only a thin woollen jumper beneath. Blue. With a faint tartan pattern. She let the jacket rest on top of the rucksack. Without the bulk of her backpack and jacket she seemed smaller. Delicate. Bright eyed. Her ponytail irritatingly bouncy. She hiked up her sleeves then lifted her voice to be heard over the commotion. 'You're confused but you need to calm down. There are a few people, I mean very few, whose DNA won't react to the frequency. That must be you. Or you would already have changed. I'm sorry to say this but you can't receive the gift.'

Boom. Throw a blanket over us and we'll cosy in then. Talk about wide eyed and slack jawed. Do we laugh. Do we cry. Do we search our pockets for a cigar. The silence was interrupted by Jason. Who'd surreptitiously wandered off to the side. He got down onto his knees to blubber at himself and paw at the grass. Sandra punctured that strange picture. She said, 'Aw for fuck sake.'

SANDRA AND JASON

There was a momentary
glow on Sandra's face
A sad joy I think
as she remembered
the good and the bad
in the days that had passed
I believe she thanked her lover
as she stood there
and wished him farewell

Jason had softened. Melting downward to the ground. His limbs flopped and his sobs spluttered into mewlings of pleasure. He let his hands rest against the ground. He breathed deeply, as if struggling to contain the happiness. Sandra's demeanour changed in the opposite direction. She hardened. Her attention moved from Jason to the woman who'd infected him. Sandra's expression went past anger. She looked ferocious. The dog reacted to this change. It bared its teeth and flattened its ears. When Sandra charged forward, her fingers were splayed outward like she had claws. The woman, rather than protect herself, grabbed the collar on the dog to prevent it from lunging at Sandra. All three collided and tumbled over the ground. The woman stubbornly held onto the dog. The dog fought against this and savagely snapped at Sandra. This kicked me into action. I stabbed the dog. Didn't think twice. Just did it. Plunging the knife into the dog was easy. Dispelling the pitch of its squeals will be more difficult. The dog died quickly, and I dropped the knife. The blonde-haired woman wasn't the only one stunned by my actions. Everyone gawped at me. Nobody noticed Ella picking up the knife. She copied me. Except she stabbed the woman. More than once, more than twice, more than three times. The blonde-haired woman tried to speak but the words came out garbled. The pool of blood that spread was terrible. It turned my stomach to look at it. Ella stood up straight and looked at me like I should've been proud of her. The woman, whose ponytail would irritate the world no longer, gurgled for a short time, then laid a hand on the dog's stomach.

ASCENSION

Lorna lifted Ella into the air
Holding her high to keep
the horror at bay
and may Ella
forever be held there
innocent and
victorious above the blood
like all the other gods of war

Joomack wanted the woman and the dog buried before the blood had dried. I was fully behind his desire for urgency. The quicker the mess was gone the sooner I could deal with erasing the images flashing through me. Sandra and Mary had taken the kids to the river. Joomack took on the job of dealing with Jason. Debbie and Lorna helped me dig the hole which was a damn difficult process. They kept placing a hand on my shoulder. Not sure if this was for my benefit or theirs. Lorna straightened. She said, 'Six feet my arse.' The laughter lifted me so quickly I felt like I'd grown wings. The elation allowed me to confront the cold calculation taking place within me. The only person infected was Jason. As far as casualties go. I could deal with that.

BURIAL

Unsettled by the sprawl of the bodies
I stepped downward to curl
their quiet forms around each other
The dog seemed smaller now
Easily able to fit
between the raised knees
and folded arms of the woman
There was something ancient
in the way we stood around the pit
I thought of all the gifts laid in graves
The tools, the jewellery, the ochre
What could I leave this stranger
Nothing. I decided
The early frost had lifted
and the day gave way to rain

Joomack had corralled Jason into the corner of the hut. Then used paracord to tie his hands behind his back and his legs at the ankles. Jason's eyes were wide and rolling. He couldn't focus and kept asking for water. Mary filled a pot. With his hands bound behind his back he was forced to lap at the water with his tongue. There were moments of clarity. Where he would blink and concentrate. In these moments he'd look at us like we were the aliens. Sandra, sensibly, was absent. She was with Lorna laying the whole shebang out for the kids. Giving it straight was the plan. No sugar. No spice. *Your Uncle Jason is an alien.* Questions would follow and they'd deal with these as they came. Debbie, Joomack, Mary and myself were entrusted with handling the practical side of the problem. This wasn't going so well. There were the hands in the pockets. There was the staring at the toes. There was many a puff of the cheek. Eventually Mary raised a finger. 'We keep'm,' she said. 'He can't infect us so where's the harm in it. We keep'm.' Debbie looked at Mary cautiously, she said, 'As opposed to what?' Joomack got down on his knees, grabbed Jason's face, and desperately asked, 'Are you in there?' Jason's eyes rolled. He said, 'I'm everywhere.'

Mary suddenly burst. The amalgamation of wrath that shot forth was one part anger and three parts truth. She pointed this in my direction. 'Why - in the name of all that is considered holy,' she shouted, 'did you murder the dug? The dug didn't need to die. The dug was just a dug. And hear this, Jason was a good man. You never gave him the respect he deserved. Well now he's your dug. And your responsibility. You take care of him.' Joomack and Debbie looked at each other like they'd won a watch. And with that I was left alone with Jason who, eyes rolling, flopped forward to lap at the pot of water.

BLASTED WONDERS

Jason is not a dug
He is one hair
on the back of the beast
that is an existential threat
to the human race
The Macallums
will gather round
this single hair
like we are lice in the pelt
Jason is not a dug
He is a pathway
to the pore that will
let us sink our teeth
into the scalp of knowledge
The aliens may have sailed
smoothly through the
vast distances in this
cruel cold universe
But now there is a
sneaky family
of blasted wonders
about to give those
big bad aliens the itch

The sun had set when Jason stopped rolling his eyes. Everyone was in the hut. This meant as he clambered toward coherent consciousness eighteen eyeballs drilled him with suspicion. He shimmied himself into a sitting position, wriggled as he tested the knots that secured his hands and feet, then said, 'These aren't tied that well. They'll come loose eventually.' He jerked his head back. 'Woh,' he said, 'You lot are much more beautiful now.' Jason confidently looked every one of us in the eye. He had smiles for the kids. A solid acknowledgement for me. He bowed slightly at Mary and Joomack and spent longer staring at Sandra. This was a mutual examination. Sandra had volunteered to speak for us. She needed the control. She got straight down to business. 'Is anyone else on their way here?' Jason replied, 'I don't know if anyone else is coming.' Sandra chose the next question carefully. 'What's happening inside you?' Jason replied effortlessly, 'Imagine trying to describe the sensation of touch to someone. To someone that had never felt it.' He shrugged. 'I can tell you it's beautiful. If everyone out there is like me, well, the world's already changed beyond what you can imagine.' He let his attention dance between us then frowned. He said, 'Where's the woman?' He answered himself, 'Aw no that's bad. What about the dog?' I replied, 'The dog's dead.' Mary looked at me with disgust. Jason spoke up, 'That woman is bound to be somebody's wife, somebody's sister.' Sandra continued that train of thought, 'We've got to assume people will come look for her. We can't be dealing with that.' Lorna embraced Ella gently. That was our cue to pull back a wee bit. Sandra said. 'I know where we can go. We'll leave in the morning.'

NOT THE SAME AS BEFORE

Last night I dreamt
of that small fire on a vast plain
Awoke to find the moon
being reflected from two points of light
bobbing and watching in the dark
Jason cocked his head at me
Then closed his eyes
returning the room to night

Didn't sleep a wink after I discovered Jason had developed the eyeshine. Freaked me out to the max. I've decided he is ma dug. Hit the tool shed this morning and knocked together a collar from an old leather belt and a padlock. The grumbles of resistance from Joomack and Mary were quickly cut when I told them his eyes glow in the dark. When I rattled the leash at Jason, he said, 'I wish you could see yourself.' What comes out when he bumps his gums together is no longer important to me. I'll be watching him like I'd watch a wolf. He'll have his hands tied as we travel and I'll be holding his leash. Can't say I'm sad to leave. Yesterday has left a stain that would stick to us if we stayed. There's positivity in the energy as we pack up. Sandra will lead us to another forest garden. One that's even more remote. I've run out of pages in this journal so I'm placing it in a toolbox and burying it with the dog. Guilt? Probably. But there's beauty in leaving it behind. I'm thinking of the hand stencils left in caves by the Neanderthals. I can feel their power now. The pigment sprayed from their lips was the language being written. The absence of their hand is the poem.

ACKNOWLEDGEMENTS

Special thanks are due to the Society of Authors for the award of a grant for work in progress. The space and time this grant provided was invaluable. I'd also like to thank the Bideford Crew (Frances, and Flashy) for the Red Bush Tea, the laughter, and the room upstairs to write. Finally, I'd like to thank Alice, for keeping me company around the fire.